To Owen,
Be SPECTACULAR!
2016

JACKSON PAYNE'S CLUMSY CHRISTMAS SPECTACULAR!

WRITTEN BY
ADAM WALLACE

ILLUSTRATED BY
JAMES HART

KRUEGER WALLACE
PRESS

Jackson Payne's Clumsy Christmas Spectacular!

First published in the year of the ninja, 2016,
by
Krueger Wallace Press

Email: wally@adam-wallace-books.com or visit
www.kruegerwallacepress.weebly.com or visit
www.adam-wallace-books.com or visit
www.facebook.com/wallysbooks or visit
The Zoo, it's really fun and there are animals. I like the big cats best.

Designer/Typesetter: James Hart
Printed in Australia by McPherson's Printing Group
Edited by Tex Calahoon

ISBN: 978-0-9944693-2-8

**Cataloguing-in-Publication entry is available
From The National Library of Australia
http://catalogue.nla.gov.au**

Do not stick this book in an elephant.
This book is not a tennis racquet or a paintbrush.

This book is dedicated to anyone who has ever given me a really good Christmas present. It's not dedicated to the people who gave me dodgy presents.

Sorry.

You brought this upon yourselves.

CHAPTER ONE

Here's the thing. The thing is, well, what I'm trying to say is … it's kind of like this.

Okay.

It's tricky to say, but I'll say it, even though everyone will hate me. Nan says it's always best to tell the truth.

So here goes.

Here *I* go.

This is me saying stuff.

Here it comes.

Ready, steady … ***spaghetti!***

Wow, this is harder than I thought it would be.

Right. It's like pulling off a band aid, and I've done that plenty of times! I just have to do it quickly, in one go.

I know, I'll practise by ***actually*** pulling off a band aid.

1, 2, 3, *OWWWWWWWWWWWWWWW!!!*

That really hurt! It's a *totally* dumb idea to pull off a band aid fast.

Owee owee ow *OW!*

Okay, I'm fine now. I'm not crying, it's just really dusty in here. I'm ready to say my piece, tell it to the world, stick it to the man.

And in 3, 2, 1 … I … don't … like … Christmas!

OWWWWWWWWWWWWWWWWW!!!

Sorry, I pulled off another band aid. Anyway, the fact is, I really *don't* like Christmas. My reason's a good one, too, because Christmas last year was an absolute disaster.

Let me tell you why.

December 24th, last year.

It was Christmas Eve, and I was *soooooo* excited. Like, *SOOOOOOOOOOO* excited!

I loved Christmas (back then). It was my *favourite* day of the year, along with my birthday, Mum's birthday, Dad's birthday, Nan's birthday, Johnny's birthday, Easter, New Year's Eve, days I didn't fall over more than five times, my first day of kinder, my first day of school, the first day Teegan Wentworth spoke to me, sunny days, rainy days, days I rode my bike, days I didn't head-butt someone and days I got chocolate chip cookies.

Christmas was the best though. Ever since I was little, like four or something, I had a routine. First, I would wake up early and empty my stocking, which would always be full of *awesome* stuff.

Then I would pack it all again, run into Mum and Dad's room, jump on their bed, say sorry to Dad for kneeing him in the guts, tip my stocking out onto their bed, say sorry to Dad for tipping stuff on his face, then describe every little thing in my stocking and why I loved it.

After that, I would run downstairs and sit on the couch until Mum and Dad came down, and we would open more presents.

Last year though, everything changed. I did all the usual stuff, even though I was 10, but after 45 seconds of sitting on the couch, Mum and Dad weren't down yet.

I was bored.

And impatient.

The presents under the tree looked really cool, especially the one at the very, very back. It was like they were whispering to me.

'Jackson. Look at us. Don't mind what the cards say, we're all for you. You should shake us and guess what's inside. Especially the one at the very, very back.'

I knew I should wait, but the freaky speaking presents made good sense. I thought I would shake one, guess what it was, and that would be it.

That would be enough.

I went for the one at the very, very back. I stepped on

three presents on the way through. I reached through the tinsel and light cords, and I got the present. Then things went wrong.

I pulled the present.

My tangled arm pulled the lights and tinsel.

The lights and tinsel pulled the tree.

I threw the present away in a panic. It knocked Mum's favourite vase off the mantelpiece and smashed it. The present landed and smashed too. It had been crystal glasses.

I started to run as the tree tipped towards me. I stepped on a present and broke it. It was a model of the Eiffel Tower Dad had spent six months making. With every step, I broke another present, and I pulled the tree further over.

I stepped on one last present.

It had roller blades in it. My left foot went through the wrapping, through the box, and into the shoe. I skated off on one leg, pulling the tree behind me.

I flew into the kitchen.

So did the tree.

I tried to stop but my leg swung around ... which meant I kicked the frozen turkey off the table ... **and out the window!** The tree burst past me and went into the fridge, stabbing all the desserts and covering them with pine needles.

I landed face first in the fruit salad.

Mum and Dad ran down to see what had happened. I could tell they were really angry, but they still untangled me and checked if I was hurt.

Mum hugged me and said it was okay. Dad hugged his broken Eiffel Tower and said, through his tears, that it was okay, that I hadn't ruined Christmas at all, not one bit.

But I had. I always broke lots of things, and now I had broken Christmas.

See? It's no wonder I hate Christmas, because I totally wrecked it! So this year, I've decided to avoid it. I will have nothing to do with it. Not one thing.

But that's not so easy when everyone else loves it so much.

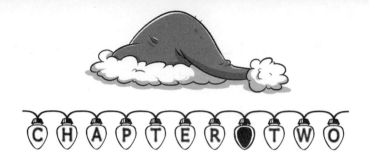

CHAPTER TWO

My first tactic, on December 22nd, was to go for a ride, get some fresh air. Mum and Dad were really getting into the spirit of things, decorating the house and the tree, wrapping presents, and it was driving me crazy.

As soon as I went outside, though, Christmas slapped me right on the butt. Seriously. Dad had redecorated my bike seat.

It wasn't any better once I rode off. Every house had decorations and lights and nativity scenes and dancing Santas. Cars had fake reindeer antlers on them. The hobo at the market had dressed up in an old Santa suit, and was yelling out stuff I couldn't understand, but assumed was something like, 'Ho! Ho! Ho! Christmas is awesome, as long as Jackson doesn't break it!'

I sighed and rode to the shopping mall. I locked my bike, I went inside, and **BAM!**

Christmas attacked me!

Christmas carols were blaring out over the loudspeakers.

People dressed as Santa's elves were handing out fliers, and shop windows had Christmas scenes all over them. There were millions of people, and they were all loaded up with potentially breakable presents.

I couldn't escape!

I ran through the mall. Kids were lining up for a photo with Santa. I accidentally bumped the kid at the end of the line, and suddenly the whole line fell like dominos.

I kept running.

Outside, the weather changed.

'Goodness,' I heard an old lady say to her husband. 'Look at that rain, dear.'

Rain, dear? Reindeer? ***AAAAGGGGHHHH!!!***

'Yes,' the old man replied. 'Well, it is Christmas, Carol.'

Christmas Carol?

NOOOOOOOOOOOOOOOO!!!

I bolted past a nativity scene. A little kid snuck in and took one of the dolls, and then started ringing the bell.

'*Noel*! *Noel*!' his mum yelled. 'Please put that doll away. Now! Put it *away in a manger*. And don't *jingle bells*. Can't we have one *silent night*?'

Was ***every*** person speaking in Christmas words? Another kid went in and started cleaning up the scene.

'Oh, you're a saint, Nicholas,' the mum said, patting his shoulder.

This was crazy. *I* was going crazy! Everywhere and everything sounded like Christmas.

I screamed and ran outside, unlocked my

bike, and rode into the rain.

It looked like I wouldn't be able to escape Christmas after all. I was proven right when I smashed into a fully decorated Christmas tree on the nature strip because I wasn't watching where I was going. It was in a pot, and I knocked it over and squished three fake elves that were under it.

I sighed, got back on my bike, and rode off, concentrating on where I was riding.

Oh well, I thought, *if I can't avoid Christmas, maybe I can pretend to totally over-the-top love it.*

Then I can be happy. Then I can make it my kind of Christmas … an accidentally awesome, blunderingly brilliant, disastrously daring, Jackson Payne clumsy Christmas spectacular!!!

On December 23rd, I woke up and I **WAS** Christmas! I leapt out of bed singing *Rudolph the Red Nosed Reindeer*. I put on green pants and a t-shirt with a picture of a Christmas tree on it. I tripped over the cricket bat I got for Christmas when I was nine.

I ran into Mum and Dad's room, jumped onto their bed, said sorry to Dad for head-butting him, and wished them both a Merry Christmas.

'Thank you, Jackson,' said Mum, 'but it's only December 23rd.'

'And it's only 3:45am,' Dad groaned, rubbing his rapidly swelling cheekbone and putting his pillow over his head. 'Go back to bed, Jackson, *please* go back to bed.'

I smiled, hugged them both, jumped off the bed, got tangled in their sheets and fell head-first onto a box of Christmas decorations that hadn't gone up yet.

I opened the box and looked inside.

Whoops.

'Go back to bed, Jackson,' Mum said. 'Get some sleep.'

'*No way, Christmas day*,' I yelled, which didn't really make sense, but it did rhyme. 'I can't sleep! It's nearly Christmas, and I *looooove* Christmas. Here's the list of presents I would like. Now I'm off to make this house more Christmassy!'

'Is that possible?' Dad asked from under his pillow. I laughed and threw my present list onto the bed then ran out of the room.

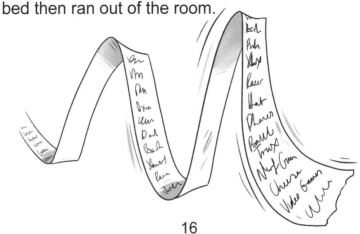

I decided the first thing I would do to make this my kind of Christmas was to help with the decorations. Mum and Dad had done really well, but I knew I could add some brilliant finishing touches.

I started by working on the Christmas tree.

Then, even though it was two days early, I set the table for Christmas lunch.

I went outside and arranged Dad's garden gnomes into a Christmas scene.

I got some breakfast, and watched Christmas shows on TV.

I went back outside and put up lights all around the outside of our house.

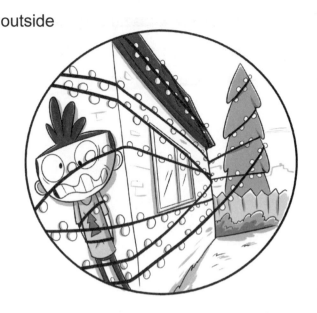

I ran down the street throwing glitter over everyone I passed.

I ran back home before the sparkly, angry mob could catch me … luckily most of them were partially blinded by the glitter that was stuck in their eyes.

I bolted through the front door, slammed it shut, and closed all the blinds. It was 10am, and I'd had a big day already.

It got bigger.

'Jackson,' Mum said as she navigated her way into the room around my decorations, 'I need to talk to you about something.'

Uh-oh. She must have seen the gnomes.

'I'm sorry, Mum. They just all looked like Santa already, so I got confused.'

Mum looked confused at my confusion. She opened the blinds just as a man blinded by glitter walked straight into the window.

Mum closed the blinds again.

'I don't know what you're talking about, Jackson, but I need to talk about *this*.'

She pointed to the Christmas tree, the table, and the food-splattered TV. Oh yeah. Mum raised a questioning eyebrow. I shrugged. Mum held out her hands, like a question. I slapped them, like I was giving her a low ten. Mum sighed and told me to *carefully* help her fix the tree.

I helped her. We finally finished at 5pm, just as Dad got home from his last day at work for the year. I knew he was home because I heard him when he saw my garden scene.

'***NOOOOOOOOOOO! GNOMEY, WHAT HAPPENED TO YOU? WHERE ARE YOUR PANTS?***'

Uh-oh.

CHAPTER FOUR

Okay. Yeah. So Dad wasn't too happy, but the really cool thing about Dad is that he gets angry for a bit, his face goes red, he clenches his teeth and hands and eyes, he stands on his toes, he makes a noise that kind of sounds like a hippo having a baby, and then he takes a deep breath and moves on. 'Jackson,' he said, once he stopped being a mumma hippo, 'I know you don't mean to be clumsy.

I do. But what were you thinking? My gnomes?'

I nodded.

'I'm really sorry, Dad, I just thought they would make a cool Santa scene.'

Dad stroked his chin.

'You do make a good point,' he said, and then he grinned. 'Luckily, I'm off work now, and I have lots of red paint in the shed. Honey, I'll be out in the yard if you need me!'

He ran outside, slamming the door behind him. I watched him go and then thought about the day. It hadn't gone so well. The good thing was, tomorrow was Christmas Eve, so I had a great chance to make things right. This could still be an *awesome* Christmas.

I woke up on Christmas Eve ready to go. First, I rode over to Johnny's house. Johnny's my best friend, and the funniest guy I know. When he opened the door though, he looked really upset. I could see why.

Johnny's Grandma loved to knit jumpers for Johnny, especially for celebrations. The problem was, she was *really* bad at knitting, so all the jumpers were dodgy as. Johnny's mum always made him wear them, though. She didn't want to upset his Grandma.

There had been the Easter jumper with the weird Easter Bunny on it; the birthday jumper that looked like the candles had set the jumper on fire; and now there was the Christmas jumper that looked like Santa had killed all the elves.

'Sorry, Jackson,' Johnny said. 'You know we always have to spend Christmas Eve with Grandma. I would really, really, really, *really* love to go for a ride with you but …'

'Johnny, time for a photo with your Grandma! She has a surprise new jumper for you!' Johnny's dad yelled from the lounge. Johnny groaned and went inside.

I rode off, and before long I came across a group of people singing carols. They had a bucket in front of them with a sign saying **DONATE** on it.

'We're practising for the show tonight,' one of them said. 'But we're also raising money for starving children who live in a desert and who can't go to school and who are orphans and who never get any presents.'

Wow. That was pretty cool. I decided to ride in circles in front of them and drum up some business.

'Come and listen to the carols!' I yelled. 'Donate money to kids who live in a school and can't have any dessert!'

Okay, so I had kind of forgotten what the

cause actually was, but it didn't seem to matter. People started putting money in the bucket. This was awesome! I was helping at Christmas! I kept riding in circles and kept yelling and the crowd watching got bigger.

Then things went a little wrong. The problem was, my toe got really itchy as I was riding around. I couldn't scratch it because I had my shoe on, and I didn't want to stop riding and yelling.

'Give money so the poor kids can have ice-cream and no athlete's foot,' I yelled, trying to ignore my itchy toe.

Then I had a brainwave! My wheel was going around pretty fast, and it had spokes on it. If I put my shoe inside the wheel, the spokes would scratch my toe and it wouldn't be itchy!

GENIUS!!!

I rode in faster circles, still yelling, and then I shoved my toe in the spokes of my wheel. It didn't quite go as planned! When I put my foot in the wheel, the wheel stopped, my bike did a front wheel wheelie, and I went flying over the handlebars.

I crashed into the singers just as they were hitting a really high note.

The note turned into a scream and I rolled off them, meaning my foot kicked the bucket of money.

It flew into the air and then landed upside down …
in the gutter … right next to a drain … so **ALL** the
money tipped down the drain!

NOOOOOOOOOOO!!!

I tried to get up to apologise, but I stood on
the hand of the person next to me. She cried out in
pain. So did the person next to her.

'No! Aria was our pianist for tonight!'

Whoops. I took another step and stepped on
someone's foot.

'No!' came the cry. 'Barney was our foot
tapper, the only person who can give us our rhythm
tonight.'

Double whoops. I went to run to my bike and
stepped on someone's face.

'*NO!* Harriet was our best singer for tonight!'

Triple whoops. I apologised heaps, but it didn't
matter. Everyone was really angry. I picked up my
bike and promised I would make things better.

No one seemed to believe me.

This was really bad.

It looked like I was breaking Christmas again.

I sat at home after that, in the backyard, and wondered what I could possibly do to make things better. This was another disaster, but I wasn't going to give up hope. No way no sir no how no way!

There had to be something I could do. I threw a tennis ball around the yard as I thought about it. One of my throws hit a window but didn't break it, so that was a win. Things were starting to look up!

I felt much better, and really started to think about how I could fix Christmas. Then I heard, from inside the house, Mum singing a Christmas Carol to herself. She poked her head out the window after the ball hit it.

'Careful, Jackson,' she said, 'and don't forget we're going to Carols in the Park tonight with Nan. So keep yourself clean and tidy, okay?'

I said I would, then stepped in a mud puddle, slipped over, and landed on my butt. I went to get up but rolled over, so now my pants were muddy on the front **and** back.

Eventually I got to my feet and realised I would have to get changed. As I walked towards the house, it suddenly hit me.

Carols in the Park!

YES!

That was it. That was where I would make everything okay again. Nan would be there, and

Johnny and his family in their weird knitted jumpers, and Mum and Dad and everyone else and even the singers for the orphans.

I started thinking about what I could do, and then I knew. The foot tapper was out of action, so I could step in for him. The singer was out of action, so I could save face by singing for her, and the pianist was out of action so I could play her part … except I had no idea how to play the piano, so that one was actually out. But I knew someone who was awesome at playing piano … *Nan!!!* She knew all the Christmas Carols too. I raced inside and rang her up, and she said she would be delighted to step in and play.

WOO HOO!

Then I searched and found the phone number of the group that was singing the carols for the desert kids, and I rang them. I spoke to Tony, the group's leader. I apologised six more times, and after half an hour he asked what I actually wanted. I told him about my plan, how I would tap and sing, and that Nan would play the piano.

Tony said he really appreciated my offer, and that if I promised not to step on anyone, I could join them. I told him I couldn't promise that, but I would do my best, and that if I *did* step on someone, I would try and not break their face like I did with the singer.

Tony said that sounded like a fair compromise, and so I was in! **YEAH!!!** Not only was I going to redeem myself and save Christmas, I was going to be the star at Carols in the Park! I might get seen by a movie producer and become a Hollywood star. I might get seen by someone from TV and become a reality TV show star. I might get seen by Teegan Wentworth, the coolest, best singing, most Christmassy girl at

our school …
if you like that
sort of thing.

This was the **BEST** Christmas ever!

CHAPTER SIX

Things started off well enough. No, really, they did. I mean, I did trip and spill apple juice all over Mr Teetee, my teacher, as he sat with his wife.

And I did accidentally bump Teegan Wentworth's mum in the back of the head with the picnic basket I was carrying.

But that sort of thing is just normal for me, so I wasn't worried. I had bigger fish to fry. I had bigger trees to chainsaw. I had bigger buns in the oven … wait … I think that means I'm pregnant.

I'm not pregnant. Let's just make that clear.

Anyway.

We found a spot to sit on our blanket, and listened to the different acts. There was heaps of stuff on for the little kids first. They all went down the front and danced and seemed to have a good time. I, on the other hand, was starting to get a little nervous. I didn't know how to tap my foot in time to music, not without kicking someone at least. I didn't know the words to many Christmas Carols either, so that was going to be a test seeing as I was the main singer.

I started to sweat.

I started to shake.

I started to dance when a choir sang *Jingle Bell Rock*.

That distracted me for a moment, but then it was time.

'Jackson,' called Tony. 'We're on in five minutes. Come and warm up with us.'

I sighed and stood up … straight on Dad's piece of cake. I stepped away and left a little cake trail behind me. Nan came too, because she was playing the piano. We joined the rest of the group and Tony introduced us. A few members glared at me, but Nan told them I was okay. That helped. She is so cool.

We warmed up, which meant we had to make weird sounds like, 'Brrrrrrrrrrrrr,' and say weird things like, 'How now brown cow.' Then we did tongue twisters, like I had to say, 'Red lorry, yellow lolly,' five times fast. It was *IMPOSSIBLE!* My tongue got so twisted I fell over! Seriously, it is *IMPOSSIBLE!*

Anyway, before long we were called to the stage. Tony gathered us in a huddle. I put my arm around Nan's shoulder and accidentally poked a lady in the eye. She squealed. I thought she was still doing a warm up noise, so I copied her, which meant I copped a one-eyed glare.

'Good luck everyone,' Tony said. 'This is a real chance to help those poor children. We'll have a bucket at the front of the stage for people to donate into. Give it your all. Let's **rock this joint!**'

We cheered and ran to the stage. Nan went to the piano. Tony handed me a microphone and guided me into the lead singer spot. It was right out the front, making me even more nervous. But this was for Christmas, and this was going to make me happy.

Tony handed me the song list. First up was *Silent Night*. Awesome. I knew that one. The problem was, I was **so** nervous my mind kind of went blank, and I totally sang the words wrong. Even my voice had gone clumsy!

This is what I sang.

'Siiiilent night.

Ghosts are white.

Did a dance, split my pants.

Everyone saw my unnnnnderwear.

Screams and shouts filled the chilly night air.

Mum put a patch on my pa-ants.

Mum put a patch on my pants.'

I closed my eyes when I finished. No one seemed to breathe. It was deadly quiet. Then someone clapped, and suddenly the whole audience was cheering and shouting and stomping their feet! People ran up and threw money into the bucket.

They loved my weird words! I turned to Tony, who shrugged. Nan gave me the thumbs up, then started playing the next song. That next song was *Jingle Bells*.

This is what came out of my mouth.

> 'Jingle bells, Santa smells,
> had baked beans to eat.
> Through the sky, this gassy guy,
> was warming up his seat, hey!'

The crowd went wild. I waved and ran around the stage with the bucket, and they filled it up.

It went on.

I sang *Ding Dong Merrily On High*.

> 'I like eating apple pie,
> Because it is so tasty!

With its soggy apple mush,

And crispy, crunchy pastry.'

It went on and on. Santa came up on stage and danced. The crowd couldn't get enough. This was it. I **WAS** Christmas. Everyone loved **ME!** I was out of control, though, and me out of control is not a good thing.

Forgetting about the wire that was attached to the microphone, I danced round and round Santa, singing my crazy words, the crowd still cheering. The problem was, I didn't realise I was wrapping Santa up like a Christmas cracker. His face went red and his arms and legs were pinned. I kept dancing.

A small child screamed.

I did a spin move and waved the microphone, but it slipped out of my hand. Because of the tightness of the wire, it flew towards Santa and whacked him right between the eyes with a thud that echoed through the loudspeakers.

Some little kids at the front started crying. I kept dancing, totally unaware of what I was doing. All I knew was that I wanted more cheers.

I tried to do a moonwalk, but I moonwalked over Tony's foot. That made me lose balance, so I reached out to grab the nearest thing I could, to try and steady myself.

The nearest thing was the Christmas tree.

I grabbed it, and I pulled it over. Santa tried to run away, but his legs were tied together so he could only do tiny jumps, and the tree came crashing down onto him, trapping him underneath it.

I ran straight into Tony, knocking him off the stage and into an old lady's lap. He clipped the bucket of money, and it wobbled. I tried to pick it up to save it. I didn't pick it up. I accidentally kicked it straight into Santa's face, knocking him out. The bucket rolled off the stage, rolled onto the ground, and went into a drain with a heavy concrete lid that just happened to have a bucket-sized hole in it.

'**JACKSON LOST ALL THE MONEY!**' cried someone in the crowd.

'*JACKSON KILLED SANTA!*' a little kid screamed, and all the children started sobbing.

'No!' I said. 'He's just unconscious. I do this to

people all the time. Look, he's fine.'

I ran over, tripped on a bauble that had fallen off the tree, and slid headfirst into Santa, head-butting him really hard ... in the head ... with my head ... which was not a good thing to do.

'*HE'S TRYING TO FINISH HIM OFF!*' the little kid screamed again, and suddenly everyone swarmed towards the stage, looking really angry, wanting to protect the jolly unconscious gift guy.

This was bad. Like, **really** bad. It looked like I actually **HAD** ruined Christmas … and possibly killed Santa.

I didn't know how I was going to get out of this one.

CHAPTER SEVEN

Suddenly, someone grabbed my shoulder. It was Nan!

'Quick, Jackson, follow me,' she said. I followed her. We snuck out the back of the stage, to where she had a Segway waiting. She got on, I jumped on next to her, and we zoomed away from the stage and the angry people.

I held on tight as Nan whizzed around a corner, haha whizz, taking me to safety. We went down some back streets and then cut around to the park. We sat on the swings, as usual, and chatted.

'Well, Jackson,' Nan said. 'You've been in some crazy situations, but I think that one took the cake.'

'There was cake?' I said. 'I didn't see cake. Is there any left?'

Nan rolled her eyes.

'Oh boy, here we go again. Now, Jackson, why were you so hyper out on the stage? What was that about?'

I told her. I always tell Nan what's going on. I said how I may have ruined Christmas last year. She agreed it had been a disaster. Gee, thanks, Nan! I stared at her, waiting for an apology. She reminded me we had eaten takeaway because the turkey had flown out the window and Dad wouldn't stop crying.

It was a fair point. I moved on.

I told her I had really wanted to be Mr Christmas this year, how even though I didn't like Christmas anymore, I thought that if I **pretended** to like it I could totally make myself happy and enjoy it more. I told her how I had tried to not break things, but had broken them worse than ever and now I wasn't happy at all and liked Christmas even less!

Nan slowly swung back and forth. I leaned forward to tie up my shoelace and tipped off the swing onto the ground. I picked myself up, sat on the swing again, and waited for Nan's wisdom.

'Jackson,' she said, 'why do you want to be happy at Christmas?'

'So I'm not unhappy,' I said.

'Okay, so why don't you want to be unhappy?' Nan asked.

I stared at her. **Really?** Wasn't it obvious?

'I don't want to be unhappy because if I'm unhappy then I'm unhappy,' I said, confident that would clear everything up.

'I want you to be happy, Jackson. I think for that to happen, though, you need to have the right intentions. A slide won't make you happy if you want to go on the swings.'

'We *are* on the swings, Nan. The slide's over there.'

Nan sighed.

'Yes, that's true. But I will tell you this. Being happy isn't just about doing things because *you* want to feel better. The true spirit of Christmas lies in the giving.'

'Oh no, you shouldn't tell lies, Nan, especially when you're giving. You told me I should always tell the truth.'

'Yes, you **should** tell the truth, but I mean lie in the sense of …'

'Taking a nap?' I interrupted. 'Like if I lie down?'

'No, it's …'

'I could use a lie down now actually, Nan. That singing and dancing really tired me out.'

Nan rubbed her face with her hands, then looked at me.

'What will make you happy this Christmas?' she asked.

I thought about that for a moment.

'If I get cool presents and don't break them and don't break anyone else's presents and don't wreck the decorations and don't make people angry and don't do the wrong thing.'

Nan nodded.

'There are a lot of don'ts there, Jackson. Did you notice that?'

51

'I don't know. I got confused.'

'I want to help you Jackson, but in the end **you** have to get this done. Only you. There's an old saying. No one can do your push-ups for you.'

'That's a good one, Nan, but I can't actually do push-ups, so someone else would **have** to do them for me.'

To prove it, I got off the swing and tried to do a push-up. It didn't go so well.

I got back on the swing, puffing and panting, and rubbing my arms.

'Jackson,' Nan said. 'I'm going to give it to you straight. If you focus on stopping bad things happening, all you are doing is thinking about the bad things all the time. Focus on the good. Focus on what you can do to help, on making others happy. If you make this a great Christmas by bringing joy to those less fortunate than you, by keeping other people in mind, then I truly believe you will come out on top.'

'Oh. Won't I squash them?' I asked.

'Squash who?'

'The people I'm keeping in my mind who I come out on top of. And how will I come out on top of them if they're in my head? Should I stand on my head? Will that do it?'

I jumped off the swings and did a headstand. Amazingly, I didn't fall over straight away. I did start laughing though.

'Hahaha, Nan, you're upside down!'

Nan stared at me.

'You're a dull boy, Jackson,' she said, then she got off the swing, jumped on her Segway, and zoomed off. I watched her go, wondering how long it would be before all the blood rushed to my head and I fell over.

OWWWWWWWWWWWWWWWW!!!

Okay, so it was about three seconds.

CHAPTER EIGHT

That night, I had a dream.

In it, I was stuffed into a Christmas stocking. Nan was playing piano, Dad's gnomes were breakdancing to the music, and Santa was somehow balancing on top of a Christmas tree. He smiled at me and spoke.

'Jackson, you are on my good list, not because of what you do but why you do it. You like helping people. Let that be enough. Think about how you can make Christmas brilliant for someone else. Take *action*. Be *awesome*. Help others. That is what will *really* make you happy. Now. Would you like some Christmas eggnog?'

I nodded and leant back my head. The tree bent down and Santa poured eggnog into my mouth. I woke up and realised I had been sleepwalking, had gone into the shower, turned it on, and was standing under it with my mouth open. I turned off the water, changed into dry clothes, and then

I knew what I had to do.

The crazy balancing dream Santa was right. If I was only worried about my own feelings, it wouldn't make things good for anyone, it would just make everyone nervous. Christmas is about giving, and I had to be the one who took the action. **Thank you, crazy balancing Santa!!!**

I checked my clock. It was 4am on Christmas morning. That meant I had heaps of time to set things right. We were doing our presents first thing, then Nan was coming over for lunch. So I had to get moving.

I emptied my stocking and put every present into a big sack. Then I raced down to the tree. First, I found all the presents that had my name on them.

There were heaps, which was **awesome**. I put them into the sack. Then I put all the presents I'd bought for everyone else into the sack too.

Next, I got all the things from my room that I didn't use anymore. I didn't put them in the sack, because it was full, but I did put them into another sack.

I ran upstairs and into Mum and Dad's room and leapt onto their bed. I said sorry to Dad for karate kicking him in the chest, wished them a Merry Christmas, and told them what my plan was. They stared at me for a moment and then broke into huge grins.

Mum gave me a big hug and they both got out of bed, had a shower, got dressed, and told me this was something they would like us to do as a family.

I rang Tony after that. At first he was angry I'd woken him up so early, but when I told him my plan he was rapt. Then I rang Johnny, and he said he would be happy to help me. He's **such** a good friend.

I rang Officer Blarney, my friend at the police station, and asked if he could help out. He said he would help as long as I didn't accidentally hurt him in some way. I said I most likely **would** hurt him, but I wouldn't mean it. He said if I didn't mean it, it would **be** accidental, which is what he asked me **not** to do. I said yeah, well duh, I knew that. He laughed and said he was happy to take the risk.

We went round to Johnny's first, and he came out of his house carrying a sack of presents. We high fived, he rubbed his face where I had accidentally high fived him, we shoved him and his sack of goods into the car, and we were off.

When we got to Tony's house, he was already up and waiting for us.

'Boys,' he said, 'this is a great thing you're doing. Let's go and change some lives.'

And that is **exactly** what we did.

CHAPTER NINE

That Christmas day was *almost* the greatest day of my life. It was just behind days I got chocolate chip cookies, but as we drove off Tony offered me a chocolate chip cookie! Then it *WAS* the best day *EVER!!!*

After leaving Johnny's we drove to the park where the disaster had happened. Officer Blarney was there with a team of friends. I accidentally stepped on his toe as I shook his hand, and he sort of gritted his teeth but moved on quickly.

'Alright, Jackson,' he said, limping to the front of the stage, which was still up from the night before. 'This is where it fell in?'

I nodded. Officer Blarney turned to his friends and nodded. They looked at each other and nodded, then moved forward. Each one took a section of the drain lid, and so did Tony, and so did Dad, and they all grunted and groaned and strained. Johnny did a fart noise, which cracked everyone up and they dropped the drain.

'Sorry,' said Johnny. 'Couldn't resist.'

Everyone said it didn't matter, it had been really funny, and then with smiles on their straining faces they lifted off the drain cover. I looked down and saw that the bucket had totally landed the right way up, and the money was still all in it!

I jumped into the drain and shoved the bucket out of it, just as Officer Blarney looked in to see if I was alright. The bucket hit him in the forehead, making him jump back. He gritted his teeth again, but didn't say anything. Mum took the bucket. I climbed out of the drain and went to see if Officer Blarney was okay. He was … until I accidentally stood on the same toe I had stood on before. He groaned and Dad said maybe it was time for us to move on.

We piled back into our car and drove to the Post Office. Tony shipped all the presents to his contact overseas, who would make sure they got to the starving children who live in a desert and who can't go to school and who are orphans and who never get any presents.

That was really cool. Especially Tony having a contact overseas. That made it seem like we were in a spy movie or something, and were shipping stolen goods to a crime boss in the mafia.

Dad looked at me.

'Jackson, did you get **all** the presents from under our tree?'

'No Dad,' I said, 'only the ones I'd bought and the ones that were for me. Oh, and the one you got for Nan.'

Dad started laughing. He said that he had bought Nan a new set of false teeth. I cracked up, imagining the lucky kid who unwrapped those!

The bank was closed, because it was Christmas Day, but the Post Office also let you deposit money like a bank. Tony put all the money from the bucket into the account for the starving children who live in a desert and who can't go to school and who are orphans and who never get any presents. He said his contact would make sure that as soon as the money was through, those kids would get the best Christmas celebration ever!

I felt so happy. This was *amazing!* Christmas was suddenly a day I could totally enjoy. I decided then and there that every Christmas from then on, I didn't want *any* presents. I would choose all the things I would like, and then we would give them to kids who never got anything.

Mum and Dad thought that was a brilliant idea, and then Johnny said he would donate his presents too!

I also decided I would sing at the carols every year to raise money. Tony didn't think *that* was such a good idea. Apparently Santa said he wouldn't make an appearance if I was singing. I thought about it for a bit, then asked if maybe I could record my part so they could play it over the loudspeakers.

Tony said he thought that would be fine.

We dropped Johnny home. His mum met us at the door and my parents told her what had happened, and what Johnny said he would like to do with his presents from then on. His mum was massively proud of him, and then said that the only present he couldn't give away was the jumper his Grandma knitted.

Johnny groaned, then groaned even more when his mum handed him a present. Johnny opened it. It was a new jumper from his Grandma. He put it on.

We all said it was very nice and then got into the car as quickly as we could before we started laughing.

After that we dropped Tony off at his place.

He got out, but looked lonely.

Mum asked what he was doing for Christmas lunch. Tony said that his family were all interstate, so he was having something on his own.

'Well,' Mum said. 'Jackson hasn't kicked the turkey out the window yet, so we have plenty to go round if you would like to join us.'

Tony's face broke into a huge grin, and he said he would love that, and that he was actually a really good cook so could help out.

Nan was waiting for us when we got home, all dressed up in her Christmas clothes. She hugged me when she found out what I had done, and said it made her so happy.

Mum and Tony cooked our lunch, which was **deeeeeelicious**, and then we spent the afternoon playing games and singing Christmas Carols to each other.

I sang *Deck the Halls*.

'Tennis balls, are green and fuzzy,

Fa la la la la, la la la la.

Bees and flies, are buzz buzz buzzy,

Fa la la la la, la la la laaaaaaaaaaaaaa!'

Adam Wallace writes a letter to Santa every year, and puts out a Christmas stocking every year. This is partly because it makes his mum excited, and partly because it makes him **REALLY** excited.

There's always a banana and an apple in the stocking.

Adam loves spending Christmas with his favourite people, and he loves eating fruit salad. He doesn't like Christmas pudding, because he hates that gross fake fruit stuff.

Find out more about Adam at

www.adam-wallace-books.com

OTHER STUFF BY
ADAM WALLACE

accidentally awesome!
BLUNDeRingLY BRiLLiaNT!
DiSaSTROUSLY DaRiNG!

HOW TO catch a LePRechaUN (NUMBeR
TWO New YORK TimeS BeSTSeLLeR!)

RhYMeS WiTh aRT
RhYMeS WiTh DRawiNG
RhYMeS WiTh caRTOONiNG

RaNDOM

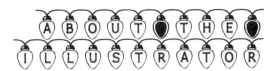

ABOUT THE ILLUSTRATOR

James Hart likes to draw, *a lot*. If his Christmas stockings aren't full of pens and pencils on Christmas morning he can get *VERY* grumpy. The only way he can be calmed down is with an over-sized block of chocolate and trifle. Mmm trifle.

James enjoys playing with his kids' new toys at Christmas and wonders why Santa stopped bringing him anything. If you see Santa, tell him James Hart the illustrator guy wants a word with him.

Find out more about James here:

www.jameshart.com.au

OTHER STUFF BY JAMES HART

accidentally awesome!
BLUNDERINGLY BRILLIANT!
DISASTROUSLY DARING!

BOY VS BEAST SERIES

YOU CHOOSE SERIES

GLENN MAXWELL SERIES

THE DAY MY BUTT WENT PSYCHO
(TV SERIES)

The iNTeRVieW aT THe BaCK oF THe BOOK

FEATURING

Crazy Balancing Santa!

Hello everyone, and welcome to **The iNTeRVieW aT The baCk Of The bOOk!**

Today we have a very special guest. It's Crazy Balancing Santa from Jackson's dream! Hello, Crazy Balancing Santa!

Crazy Balancing Santa: Well, hello ho ho there, young man. It's good to see you.

It's good to see you too, although do you have to be balancing on top of the angel on top of the tree?

Crazy Balancing Santa: Ho ho ho, of course I do, sonny! I am a balancing Santa from a dream. I'm always balancing.

Okay then, well that's great. Now, in Jackson's dream, you gave him some good advice. Does that mean you're on the nice list and not the naughty list?

Crazy Balancing Santa: Oh, I'm always on the nice list … except for that one time I was balancing on top of thirty two crystal champagne glasses. That didn't end well.

No, I bet it didn't. Smashed all the glasses huh?

Crazy Balancing Santa: No, not one of them. But I did spill the champagne, and the Easter Bunny wasn't happy about that.

Riiiiight. Well then, the breakdancing gnomes in the dream. Friends of yours?

Crazy Balancing Santa: Ho ho ho, yes indeed they are!!! Lovely gents, grow a fine beard, they do. You know what they always say … a good beard means a good heart.

They say that?

Crazy Balancing Santa: Well, I say that.

Good enough for me, you're Santa!

Crazy Balancing Santa: Ho ho ho!

Well said. Hey! How are you suddenly on a tightrope above the Grand Canyon?

Crazy Balancing Santa: A) I'm Crazy Balancing Santa, and B) this whole interview is a dream.

Ooooooooh. Spooky. So can I pinch myself to wake up?

Crazy Balancing Santa: You can try.

Okay. And OWWWWWWWWW!

Crazy Balancing Santa: Whoops, sorry, I forgot, this isn't a dream. My bad.

Thanks Crazy Balancing Santa, you're a great help. Now Santa, I would like to try some word association. So I will say something, and you say the first thing that pops into your head.

Crazy Balancing Santa: Very good. But first, would you like a candy cane?

Yes please. Mmmmm, that's good. Okay, here we go. Word association with Santa. Motorbike gangs.

Crazy Balancing Santa: Excellent beards.

Yosemite Sam.

Crazy Balancing Santa: Fine moustache.

Gandalf the Great from Lord of the Rings.

Crazy Balancing Santa: Copied my style.

And finally, the seven dwarfs.

Crazy Balancing Santa: Dopey should have grown a beard.

Crazy Balancing Santa, who is now riding a unicycle on top of a flagpole, thank you for joining us at The iNTeRview aT The BaCK Of The BOOK!

Crazy Balancing Santa: HO! HO! HO! Merry Christmas everyone, and sweet dreams!

also available

also available

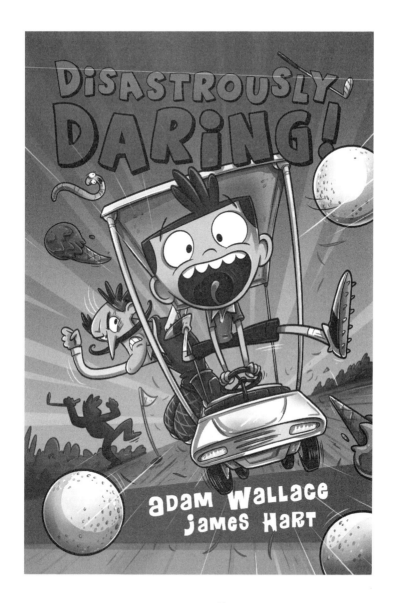

ALSO AVAILABLE